The Story Snail

F. Rockwell

For Nicholas, Julianna, Nigel,
and Christian—A. R.

To Jason—T. S.

3062 00004 0543

Text copyright © 1974 by Anne Rockwell
Illustrations copyright © 1997 by Theresa Smith

Simon & Schuster Books for Young Readers
An imprint of Simon & Schuster Children's Publishing Division
1230 Avenue of the Americas
New York, NY 10020

Also available in an Aladdin Paperbacks Edition.

The text of this book was set in Utopia.
The illustrations were rendered in oil pastels and colored pencil.
Printed and bound in the United States of America

10 9 8 7 6 5 4 3 2 1

The Library of Congress has cataloged the
Simon & Schuster Books for Young Readers Edition as follows:
Rockwell, Anne F.
The story snail / by Anne Rockwell ; illustrated by Theresa Smith.
p.   cm. — (Ready-to-Read)
Summary: John can do nothing well until a snail gives him one hundred
fabulous stories to tell, but when even they wear thin, he goes in search
of the snail again.
ISBN 0-689-81221-3 (hc)   0-689-81220-5 (pbk)
[1. Storytelling—Fiction. 2. Self-confidence—Fiction. 3. Snails—Fiction.]
I. Smith, Theresa, ill. II. Title. III. Series.
PZ7.R5943St   1997
[Fic]—dc20   96-19215   CIP   AC

The Story Snail

By Anne Rockwell
Illustrated by Theresa Smith

Ready-to-Read
Simon & Schuster Books for Young Readers

Chapter One

Once, long ago, there was a boy named John. John was good and kind, but he could not do anything well. Nothing at all. And everyone laughed at him. So one day he ran away. He ran away to the meadow and hid in the tall grass.

"Pssssst!" said a little voice. John looked everywhere, but he could not see anyone.

"Here I am," said the little voice. A snail with a silver shell was sitting on his shoe.

"I am a magic snail," it said. "I am the Story Snail. Because you cannot do anything well but are good and kind, I will give you a gift. I will give you one hundred stories no one has ever heard before. And whenever you tell a story, everyone will listen. 'How well he tells stories!' everyone will say."

And the snail told John one hundred stories. Then it crawled away.

GREAT STORY!

Chapter Two

John went home. He told the first story just the way the snail had told it to him.

"That is a good story!" everyone said. "Tell us another story, John."

And John told another story. Every

day John told a story. He told stories
until he had told every story the snail
had given him.

"Tell the stories again!" the boys and
girls said.

And John told the stories again and again and again—until one day a little girl said, "Oh, tell us a new story. I have heard that story before."

"I do not know a new story," said John sadly.

And everyone laughed and said, "John tells the same stories over and over again. They are boring."

"I must go and find that magic snail and ask it for a new story," John said to himself. He went back to the meadow. But the snail wasn't there.

Chapter Three

John called the snail but it did not
answer. He did not know what to do.
"Whooooooo, wheeeeeeeee," he
heard suddenly. "I am the Wild West

Wind. The snail is far away. You will
never, never find it. You had better go
home. Whooooooo, wheeeeeeee."
And the Wild West Wind blew John's
hat away.

But John would not go home. He walked and walked until he came to a dark forest. In the forest John saw a green elf. "Have you seen a snail with a silver shell?" he asked.

"Once I saw that snail," the elf said, "but I do not know where it is now. It gave me one thousand stories. But because I did not tell them to anyone, they all turned to mushrooms!"

"Mushrooms?" said John.

"Yes, mushrooms," said the elf sadly. "All the mushrooms growing in this dark forest are the stories I did not tell. And the snail has never come back again."

"I can't tell you where it is," said
the elf, "but I will give you a magic
password. You never can tell, it may
come in handy." And he whispered to
John, "Fuzzbuzzoncetherewas."

Chapter Four

John walked on until he came to the blue sea. He saw a mermaid sitting on a rock. "Have you seen a snail with a silver shell?" John asked.

"No," said the mermaid. "But I can tell you what the sea horse told me. He has seen the snail with the silver shell."

"Tell me, please tell me!" said John.

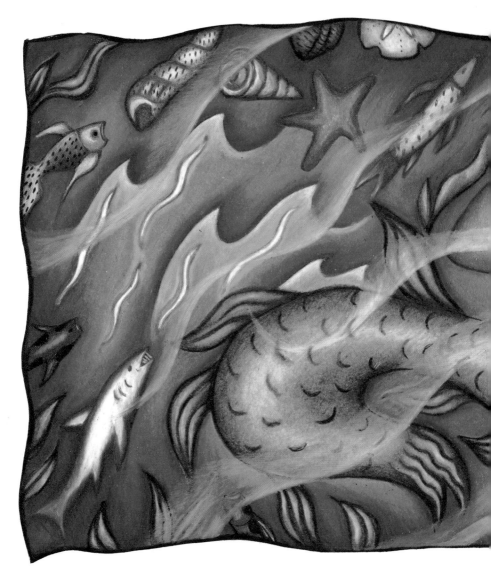

"You must do a kind thing and a brave thing, and you must have a magic password. Then you will find the snail with the silver shell. That is what the sea horse told me."

"I have a magic password," said John.
"The elf gave it to me. If you tell me
what to do I will do it."

But the mermaid swam away.

John walked on. He came to a garden.
A little rabbit was sitting in the garden.
It looked sad. "Have you seen the snail
with the silver shell? Do you know
where it is?" said John.

"How would I know where it is? I do
not even know where I am. I am lost,"
said the rabbit. And it began to cry.

"Don't cry," said John. "I will try to
take you home. Where do you live?"

The little rabbit said, "I live at the
edge of a dark forest. It is where the
green elf lives. A thousand mushrooms
grow there. It is far away."

"Poor me," thought John. "I have
come so far, and now I must go
backward. I will never find the
snail now."

He picked up the lost rabbit and patted
its fur. "I will take you home," said John.
"I have just come from that forest. I
know where it is." And he took the little
rabbit home to its mother.

"You have done a very kind thing,"
said the mother rabbit, and she gave
John a carrot.

"Have you seen the snail with the silver
shell? Do you know where it is?" said John.

23

"I have never seen it, but I have heard it from inside my rabbit hole," said the mother rabbit. She pointed to a big rock and said, "Behind that rock there is a cave, and in that cave lives the snail with the silver shell."

"What have you heard?" said John.

"I have heard words, words, words," said the mother rabbit. "Have some lettuce." But John ran to the rock.

Chapter Five

John pushed the rock away.
Something was growling in the deep,
dark cave. "That is not the snail with
the silver shell," thought John. He was
afraid, but he went into the cave. He
saw a bright red fire. Then he saw a
big green dragon.

"Grrrrrr!" said the dragon. "Who are you? I do not like the looks of you. I might as well eat you up!"

"Please don't," said John. "I am John, and I have come to find the snail with the silver shell."

"I know that snail," said the dragon.
"It lives in this cave with me, but it
will not tell me any stories. It says I
spit fire and growl and eat things up.
I will not let you find it." And the
dragon growled.

"If I tell you a story," said John, "will you let me see the snail?"

"No!" said the dragon, and he growled again.

"Two stories?" said John.

"No!" said the dragon, and spit fire.

"Ten?" said John.

"One hundred!" shouted the dragon.

And so John told the dragon all the stories the snail had given him. And the dragon did not spit fire or eat John up. The dragon growled softly as he listened.

When John had told the last story, the dragon said, "Walk ten steps forward. Take twenty jumps to the right. Take one giant step backward. Close your eyes and jump three times. Open your eyes and you will see a golden door. Knock once loudly and twice softly. Then say the magic password."

"And what is that?" said John.

"I do not know," said the dragon sadly. "The snail will not tell me." But John knew.

hello snail

Chapter Six

John walked ten steps forward and took twenty jumps to the right. He took one giant step backward, closed his eyes, and jumped up three times. When he opened his eyes he saw a

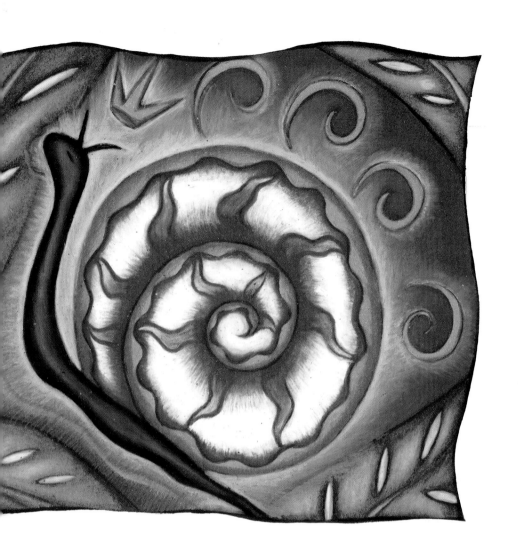

golden door. He knocked once loudly
and twice softly. Then he said,
"Fuzzbuzzoncetherewas!" The golden
door opened, and John saw the snail
with the silver shell. It was eating a
green leaf.

"Hello, snail," said John. "I have come to ask you for a new story. I have told all the stories you gave me. Even the dragon has heard them. No one wants to hear them again."

The snail stopped eating. It looked at John and poked out its little horns.

"I cannot give you a new story," the snail said.

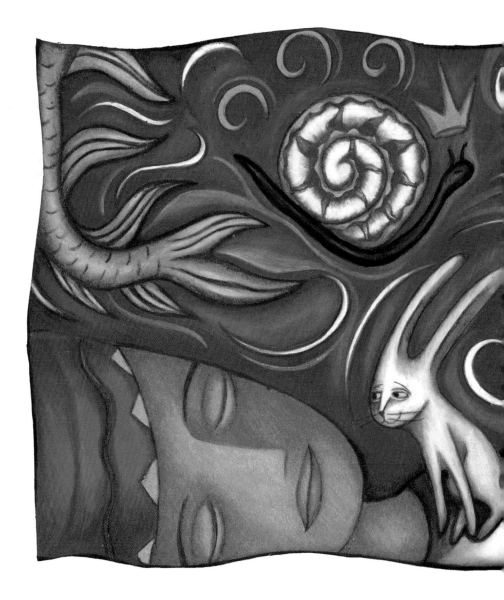

"There are many new stories to tell, that is true. But now you must find them for yourself. You have come so far, though, that I will send you

safely home."

Softly the snail whispered,
"Fuzzbuzzoncetherewas!" and John
fell asleep at once.

Chapter Seven

When John woke up he was home.

"Have you found a new story, John?" everybody asked. But John had no new story to tell. Then he heard a bee buzz. Suddenly John smiled. He said, "Fuzzbuzzoncetherewas a boy named John. John was good and kind, but he could not do anything well. Nothing at all. Everyone laughed at him. So one day he ran away."

And John told about the magic snail with the silver shell, the Story Snail. He told about the Wild West Wind and the green elf. He told about the mermaid and the lost rabbit. He told about the dragon in the deep, dark cave.

John told the story you have just read. And after that, whenever he wanted to, John told a new story.

And everyone said, "John tells stories very well indeed!"